S0-AFN-323

THE HIDDEN INFINITIES

Stories and Art
Gustavo Alberto Garcia Vaca

contents

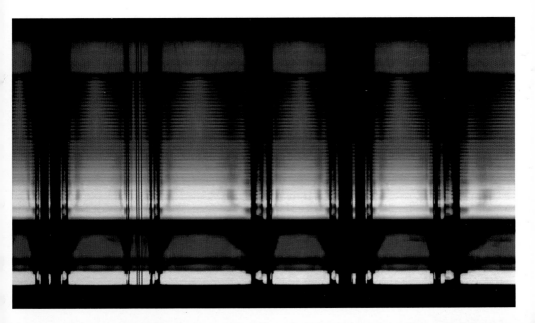

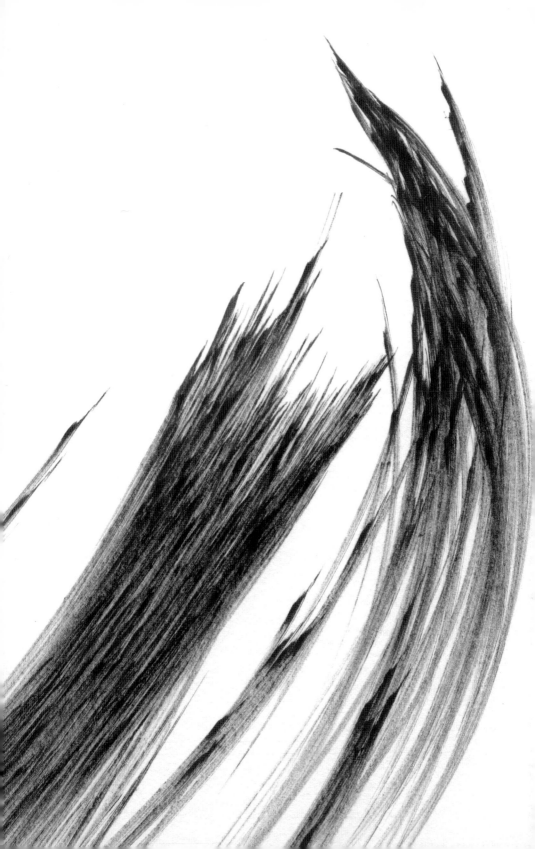

Orisha

I awoke. Sleep had been marked with circles of swimming bodies. My hands slithered into the cool river. I stretched into the sunlight, the rays surrounding me, ringing in my ears. The morning wind ran through my feathers - I felt myself shiver. Her usual anxiousness at the beginning of a new world. The clouds were heavy under our feet. Her plumage rattled and the scales of my hands arched in time around her. Her dark eyes held the mysteries of endless life and I gazed inside as we walked.

All of us spread across the sky to form a shield, a shelter, for the creatures below. The weight was steady, at times unbalanced, always secure. My shoulders caught the axis of the previous night's prayers. Thousands of voices, each asking for sustenance. My back arched, my arms thrown upwards. Millions of words slipped down my trembling spine. She extended her smooth-leafed hands, catching each one, breathing them in and sending out wisps of cool, fragrant light to fall upon their faces, smiles spreading among them.

My brother cast his part of the sky high over his head and dove down towards the depths of the wooded animal that was their home. His blue body was a sharp, glimmering jewel descending. I felt the sky ripple in his absence, greyness flooding in from where his iron frame had stood.

I glanced above us, towards our father and mother, guiding the caravans of spirits. I looked across the expanse of the weight upon us. I imagined their soft souls looking up towards us, their hopes forming avalanches that swirled upwards. Her hands soothed my spine, tracing symbols up and down my back - the symbols that drip down into their thoughts as they sleep.

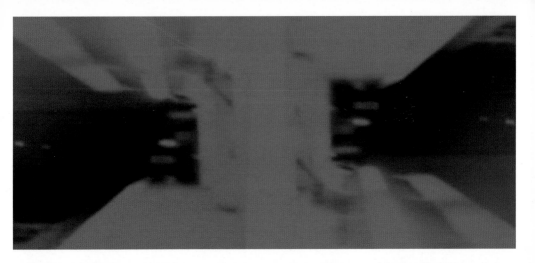

The Furthest Colony

Cloud-form and spiral-shape galaxies pass across the monitors. I look out to the suns, the planets, the days, the cycles of others. I picture Lia in my mind, back at Seri Station, going through the data that I have been transmitting for her to analyze. A coldness washes over me, sharp, yet comforting in some way. I look towards the Sinu galaxies. When I was younger, I had memorized the arrangement of stars there: I had always been drawn to their thin, veiled shapes. And now here I am, seeing them before me. I slowly scan across the stars, savoring their calming light.

My vessel reaches the edge of the Thera Black Hole. I arrive at Apache Station colony just as the Kuna moons begin to set. I transmit my greeting code but get no response. I keep trying, sending variations of the code. Nothing. I signal Seri Station that I will now attempt to board. I move towards the docking bay of Apache Station, the furthest colony we have created. And the costliest experiment in history for developing a new energy source, an experiment that seems to have gone wrong.

No one from Seri Station has had any contact or response from anyone on Apache Station for a week. It is believed that everyone could have died in one of their experiments. I took this assignment thinking this would be my only opportunity to venture out to this distant area of space during my lifetime.

The docking bay is still. No sign of recent use. I leave my vessel, camera in hand. I begin searching the station. On the communications deck I find broken transmitters, smashed screens. But no crew. I speak to Seri Station - they can see everything I am recording. The image signal is sharp.

I continue onto the control deck. The only sound is the electronic hum of a decaying frequency. I inspect the signal: it is feedback from the station's own instruments. I shut it off. I turn to the control boards. I see Doctor Samuel, slumped over his boards. "Doctor Samuel?" I whisper. He lifts his head and faces me. His face is sad, as if he has been crying.

"You will tell them what has happened here," he tells me quietly.

I approach him cautiously. "Doctor Samuel, are you all right?"

"You will return here again soon."

"What has happened here?"

"You will tell me your name is Tuos," he states blankly.

"My name is Tuos. It is an honor to meet you, Doctor Samuel." I extend my hand but he only stares at it.

"Who...? Who is...? I am.... I will not...remember."

"You will not remember? What do you mean? Please tell me what happened here." I sit near him, setting the camera on a control board.

"You will ask me a series of questions." He looks at me, but he is looking beyond me, through me, as if he is looking into space.

"Doctor Samuel, what has happened here? Where are the other scientists? Where is Doctor Philips? Doctor Clark? Or Commander Elm? Commander Sun? Where is everyone?" I try to engage his eyes, but he continues looking through me.

"You will travel here again. With Lia. I will not survive the trip back to Earth," he says solemnly. He then slumps over, his head hitting the control boards with a loud crash. I lift his head. He has fainted. I try to wake him, but he only mumbles and throws his head back onto the control boards. I check the energy data from the Thera Black Hole. There are streams of unanalyzed data: I transmit all of this data to Seri Station. I leave him for now and go to the pod bay - every pod has been jettisoned. I search the boards for their destinations. Every pod was programmed to the center of the Thera Black Hole.

Scared, I move quickly to Apache Station's calculation deck. I look into the monitors. In the nearby Thera Black Hole I begin to see a shape I have never seen before. I direct the monitor to zoom in. There seem to be streaks of orange light angling from the edge of the black hole, spinning off in many directions. There appear to be many levels, many planes of light distinctly split. Are they x-ray or gas emissions? But the planes of light are sharp and definite. The light is spreading in some type of pattern. My heart beats hard inside my chest as I look into something I have no concept of. My fingers tremble as I quickly contact Seri Station: they are also recording this occurrence, and also have no idea of what this is or what is happening.

Just then, I notice that the brightness of the angles of light is growing. I watch the brightness grow into a deep orange light, which then releases its energy throughout the many angled planes. The energy travels across each plane at a different speed and brightness. Space itself seems to be illuminated for a moment in a blast of light.

My body shakes. I do not know what is happening. I cannot understand why the doctors would have left Apache Station. Why would they have gone into the Thera Black Hole, into their own almost certain destruction? I do not know what has happened to Doctor.... Doctor...? What is his name? Doctor...? I cannot remember his name right now. I must be in shock. I run back to the control deck. I try to wake him up, "Doctor..., Doctor...." He opens his eyes slightly, mumbling. He does not get up. I carry him to my vessel and anxiously prepare for takeoff. I have the sense that something is beginning...or ending. I try to take deep breaths. I program my vessel towards Seri Station and take off.

I move through space, away from the black hole. I feel that I am in some new place. Space seems different, brighter, at points. I pass galaxies whose names... that now... I cannot... remember.

I contact Seri Station. "Hello, is this...? This is.... Yes, I...I think I.... Who is....this? Lia? Who is...Lia? I'm sorry...I can't...."

I hear a woman's voice, calling a name that sounds familiar. "Tuos, are you there? It's me, Lia. It's me! Tuos, what's happening?" I do not know what to say to this person, so I hang up. I realize that soon I will return to this station, with the woman I just spoke with, and with others. And we will find that the black hole cannot be used as a reliable energy source, but that it is....

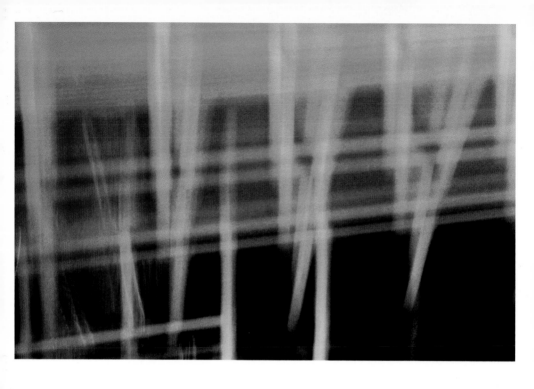

Journey's End

Isis looked out of her glider's small windows. She could see the rows of buildings beneath the surface of the waters. Smoke rose up from the floating encampments that stood a few feet above the rippling water. She sensed movement in the black skies above and lowered her head in prayer. The glider soared over the crystalline waters, over the hundreds of encampments and rafts. Isis could see people waving at her. Isis smiled and waved back. Even though she did not know them, she and the others had heard their pleas, calling for her to save them.

Isis remembered her father. The way his eyes would brighten when he smiled. She was here now because of him - because he had taught her to see, to listen. Isis looked to the faint glow of the sun. She was born after the oil wars, after the bomb detonations, after the sun became a dim light in the black skies. She remembered how her mother would describe what real sunlight felt like, what trees sounded like in the breeze.

The glider flew automatically. Voices called to her and she closed her eyes, listening. The glider turned south, heading deeper into the continent. She felt the oncoming radiance. She viewed the monitors, seeing the ashes below, the smoldering earth. She could see the valleys within the black sand dunes. The glider descended, landing with a coarse, rolling sound. She placed the

oxygenated mask unit over her face and took her computer transmitter. A blast of wind struck her as she stepped out of the glider. The sand crackled under her feet. The dunes extended into the horizon. She kneeled, listening.

Voices chanted within the winds. The black skies swirled above her. She walked for hours, then stopped. The voices became whispers. She began excavating. The weight of the sand grew heavier with each movement. Her breath grew faster within her oxygenated mask unit. She felt a thin wooden box and pulled it from the ground.

The voices stopped. Her hands trembled as she opened the box. The disk shimmered against the black sand. She had been guided to the ancient data: she prayed in gratitude. She placed the disk into the computer transmitter. Texts and formulas streamed across the screen. Her eyes lit up as the ancient knowledge was downloaded. She began transmitting this data to the world networks, to those who, like her, had been waiting their entire lives for this moment. When the transmission was complete, she bowed, in silence, waiting.

The dark skies parted - revealing a brightness she had never experienced, colors she had never seen. She felt herself smile as an unknown sunlight spread across the dunes, and the earth.

The Momentary Labyrinth

Years ago, the king of a distant land ordered a new palace built for himself. It was built upon terrain that had previously been only sand. The palace structure was made of high walls, and windows that allowed the white light of the region to enter the many chambers inside. On the palace grounds, courtyards, paths and lagoons were created.

Among the palace grounds, the king also had a labyrinth built, from his own designs. The labyrinth was vast and complex, with innumerable corridors and galleries. The walls of the labyrinth were as high as the walls of the palace itself. The king had always wanted to build a labyrinth, for as long as he could remember. He had created many designs over the years, and ultimately decided to build the design in which the entrance faced towards the setting sun. The king felt a deep sense of accomplishment at having fulfilled his life's wish. He would happily spend hours each day getting lost

within the series of dark, narrow passageways.

       When the king would receive guests from other kingdoms, he would proudly show them the labyrinth. Many guests would remark that it seemed to rise from the desert sand like a dream. He would enjoy seeing their amazement at the complexity of his creation. Some guests would enter the labyrinth, only to quickly run out in fear. Others would walk in, and return much later with a deep calm in their eyes. For those who were frightened by the labyrinth, their time in it seemed as though many days and nights had passed. For those who walked through the labyrinth's many corridors, the time that passed felt like a few seconds.

       The king would laugh at his guests' varying responses, knowing that one day he would enter the labyrinth and not exit.

Evolution

The trees call out in orange flames, their red-leafed tongues striking at the wind. The machinery of our movement glides in smooth muted sound. The calls of the trees reverberate through the glass. We glide in our silver vehicle under the falling dusk, rising into the darkening cliffs.

We reach the wooden house, its ancient form calming our thoughts and erasing the city and the spreading hysteria. Music plays through the audio-sensors. The repetition over and across memories and wood. The walls of records, sounds held within walls whose roots reach inside these memories and pull them forward into the present: the pains and overcoming, the joy and selection.

Evening grows around us. Outside - a web of bright seconds, the taste of hummingbird flutterings in the ocean breeze. Outside - sirens and callings, searchlights and twilight. The distant sounds of streets untying themselves in madness.

The voices of the trees become whispers under the full moon. Inside, the night becomes its own season. Ola's voice crosses to the window, parting the curtain, opening memories in a sweet, brilliant flash. We hold each other in the evening breeze. Ola's words find their way through the stacks of papers, charts and silent photographs. The remains of our previous escape. We find comfort in the shards of our previous marks of time.

We look out, the sounds of the trees now silent. A star falls in brightness, the treasures of these moments buried in its sands. We turn back to our home, now a refuge. We begin to barricade all the doors and windows. We fall asleep, wrapped in each other's arms and locked into our orders.

Morning falls across the coast. We switch on our computer systems, listening to the day's reports. The sickness has been reported throughout Europe and the Middle East. Massive ice storms are now striking all of Western Europe. The sickness has been detected along the coasts of Africa and India, which are both still in a state of emergency due to the hurricanes that continue to strike. The coasts of most Asian countries are still completely flooded after the tsunamis that hit last month. It has been confirmed that the sickness has spread to every country in North and South America. The death toll from last week's earthquakes throughout the entire Western Hemisphere is now in the millions.

We begin reading the data from the hundred new Skyphozoan units we launched yesterday morning. We calculate and chart the findings. Nothing has changed from the previous readings. Ola programs the robotic Skyphozoan units to swim out another 5 kilometers. We watch the coastal camera monitors as the blue lights of the Skyphozoan units flicker further out into the ocean. Their jellyfish-like bodies glow in the deep green waters. When the lead Skyphozoan unit reaches the 5 kilometer point, we switch on its camera. Sludge, seaweed, waste. The visibility is worse than we imagined. Simultaneously, the Skyphozoan units descend into the ocean canyons, searching. We watch in disgust as thousands of dying fish, dolphins and seals swim past the camera. Dr. Singh's findings off the coast of southern India last week confirmed that the world's ocean plant and animal life was all dying of the same disease. Finding the source of this disease is why we're here. Why we were ordered into service.

Ola programs 20 of the Skyphozoan units to recheck samples from the dying fish and sea animals. I contact the World Disease Commission with today's findings and report our decision to search deeper in the ocean canyons.

The blue light of the lead Skyphozoan unit burns through the thick ocean waters. Its robotic body maneuvers through the thousands of dying creatures, diving deeper into the darkness. Ola turns on the thermal imaging circuits in its dome-shaped body. There appear to be red glowing areas along these canyons, signaling the presence of concentrated Dysecium, which is believed to be the toxic chemical responsible for the spread of the most devastating pandemic the earth has ever experienced.

The lead Skyphozoan unit reaches the canyon floor and Ola nervously programs all the units to fan out across this canyon system, one beginning from each end of each canyon. The units' long tentacle instrumentation spread across the canyon walls, data streaming back to our computers. I turn and watch Ola's eyes, excited, yet afraid.

The 20 Skyphozoan units have rechecked the fish and animal samples, transferring the data to Ola's computer. We read through the data - the data is the same. It is the same disease that Dr. Singh confirmed to be afflicting every country on the planet. The same disease that Ola and I first discovered, just two weeks ago, here in Soledad Bay. Here, on the coast where Ola and I would come to find peace from our professional responsibilities. Here is where we found the highest source of Dysecium on the planet.

I remember how the madness seemed to spread faster after the day we discovered the disease began here. In large cities, murders and riots seemed to increase. Hundreds of thousands of plants, animals and humans continue to perish each day. The effects of this disease are incalculable. And the source of Dysecium is still unknown. We are all hoping to find it before it's too late. We hope there is some way to create a cure before the earth, as we know it, dies.

Blue light cuts through the sludge flowing back and forth on the canyon floor. The sludge surrounds the lead Skyphozoan unit's camera: Ola programs the unit to rotate its body to clear away some of the sludge. The unit's thermal imaging circuits begin reading the red glowing areas, the thermal images growing brighter. I open the charts to view our calculations of the levels of Dysecium that could have caused this disease. The lead Skyphozoan unit's tentacle instruments reach out to the source of the brightest red glowing area. The camera is clouded with waste. Ola programs the unit to rotate again. The red glowing area is seen through the camera to be butterfly coral.

Ola and I face each other. We cannot speak. Butterfly coral is the source of the Dysecium. Butterfly coral is the source of the disease. Like all of the world's coral, butterfly coral was long thought to be completely extinct. Yet here are a few coral, here in Soledad Bay. The lead Skyphozoan unit's tentacle instruments read the Dysecium levels on the surface of the coral. I chart the data - the Dysecium levels are beyond any that have been recorded anywhere. Through the camera we can see that the coral is dying, and it is releasing all of its chemicals, including the toxic Dysecium, into the water. Into the ocean currents that are carrying the poison to every shore of every continent of the world.

The lead Skyphozoan unit continues sending the chemical data, the data sequence streaming across our computer monitors. Ocean waves continue crashing on the shore, the sounds echoing across the cliffs.

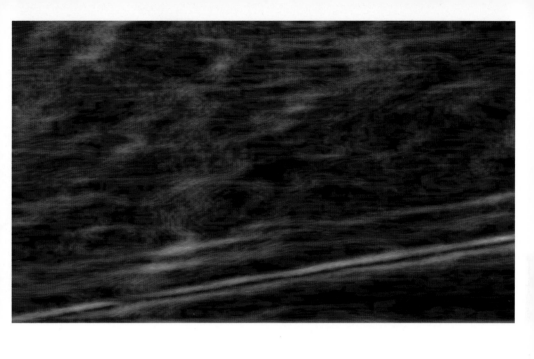

Visitation

The rain caught it by surprise. The morning had been so clear. The blueness of the sky seemed as vast as memory. Then, out of nowhere, gusts of wind, sheets of rain. The drops fell with force, striking the earth in front of it. It moved forward and entered a cafe. It felt their eyes watching it, some with fear, others feeling calmness. It moved to a dark corner in the back. Its glow of light emanated from the corner of the dimly lit cafe. There were many people in the cafe. Some of them, noticing that it would not be leaving, quickly paid their bill and left. Most stayed, enjoying its glow and watching the rain on the other side of the cafe windows. Most of the people in this town were welcoming to it, as many people around the world were. The song playing in the cafe speakers was from another era, and seemed to complement this day - the blue morning, the torrents of rain. On the floor, squares of red tile led across the narrow length of the cafe. Its glow illuminated the tiles as it moved back outside.

The rain soon stopped. Puddles formed shapes of light along the sidewalks. The streets were quiet. It approached the town's small train station. Children silently watched it move by them. A cat ran through its glowing light, purring. A train arrived and people soon rushed by it, many of them smiling. Sounds of their footsteps echoed across the metal platforms. Across the tracks were houses and trees in the distance.

Another train approached, the platform trembling. Sparks reflected in the puddles of rain water beneath the rails. It boarded the train. Outside, small towns and farms blurred past. The sky was clearing. It sensed the peace that now resided in this area. Its time here was complete. Its glow dissipated, its sparks reflecting on the train windows.

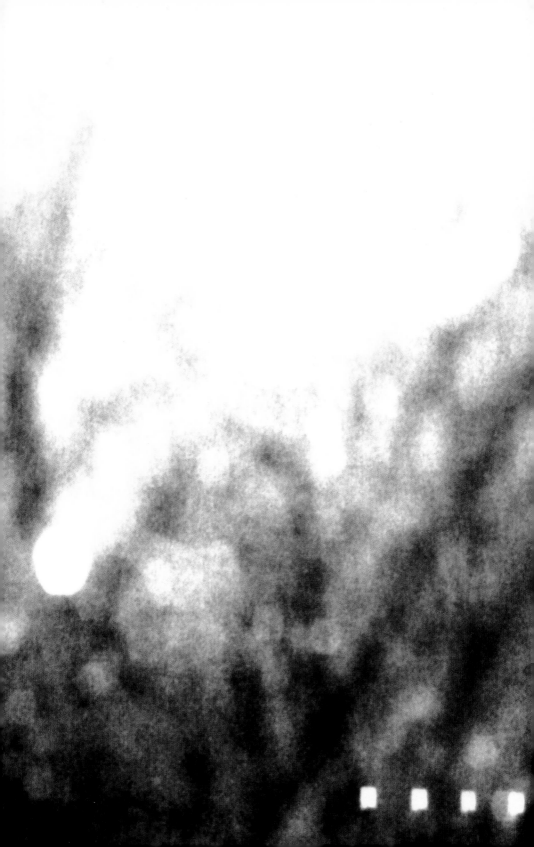

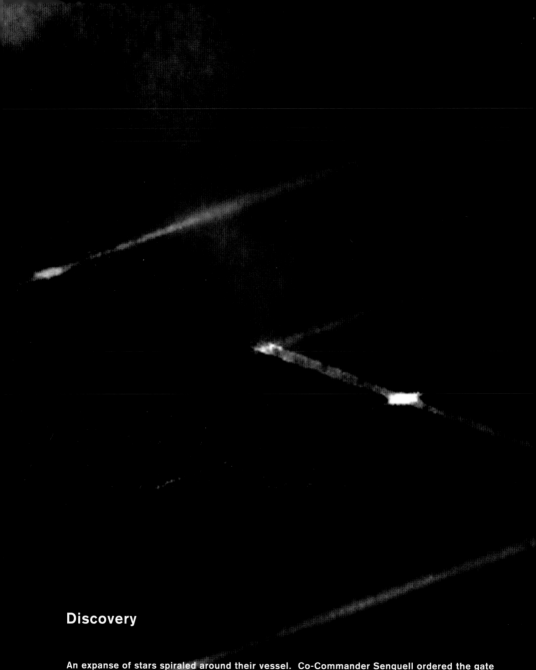

Discovery

An expanse of stars spiraled around their vessel. Co-Commander Senquell ordered the gate propulsion program onto the main screens, his eyes fixed on the spreading star clusters. Coordinates and sequences appeared on the main screens, with each crew member referencing and encoding data. Deep rumblings shook the command deck as their vessel, the Gama, entered the gate propulsion phase. A shock of fear coursed across their faces, then subsided: such a jolt was to be expected. The main screens showed all levels stable. Starlight left thin streaks across the irises of Senquell's eyes. The first human mission out of their galaxy. The first human eyes to behold another planetary system.

The second crew was awakened: they prepared themselves then walked to the command deck to relieve the first crew. Co-Commander Nisa took her place on the command deck as Senquell walked slowly to his chamber. The small white stars of their country's flag hung above him. Senquell

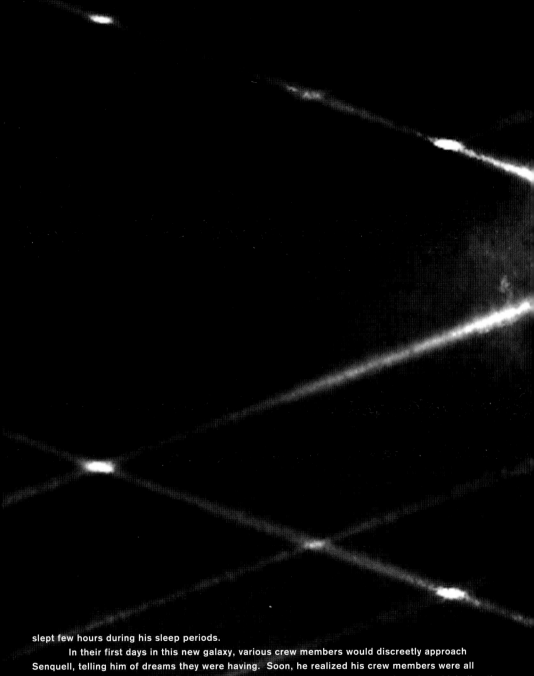

slept few hours during his sleep periods.

      In their first days in this new galaxy, various crew members would discreetly approach Senquell, telling him of dreams they were having. Soon, he realized his crew members were all having similar dreams - of walking alone through a vast jungle landscape, not knowing which direction to go. Fear began to spread among the crew as they discovered they were having similar dreams. Senquell conferred with Nisa - neither of them were having such dreams. Nisa confessed to sleeping very little during her sleep periods. They decided to run brain scans on all of the crew members: the scans showed normal results in all of them. Senquell and Nisa assured their crews that their dreams were subconscious reactions to this completely new and different environment.

      By the twenty-fourth day, crew members' fears caused by their continued dreams began to impede their work. Senquell and Nisa contacted Earth. Central Control sent psychological tests for

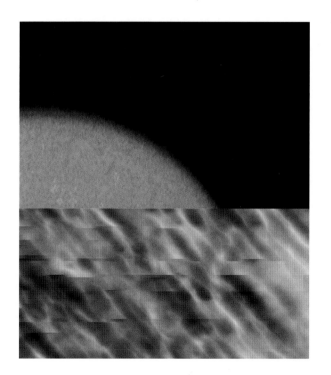

them to complete. They sent the completed tests back to Earth. The analyses showed no abnormalities in any of them. Everyone was operating in accordance with their profiles. The Gama was following its trajectory in the specified time. Everything was moving as planned. The orders were to continue with their excellent work. These words from Earth eased them as they moved deeper into this unknown galaxy.

In their respective sleep periods, Senquell and Nisa began to sleep more. Senquell soon began to dream, first seeing fields of dark colors, which then took the shape of a green jungle landscape. He spoke privately with Nisa - she had also begun to dream of being alone in a jungle. Neither of them had ever been to such a place on Earth. They rationalized that the crew members' dreams had convinced their own subconscious to reference this unknown star system to a place on Earth. Nisa and Senquell assured each other of this and decided not to tell their crews of their dreams.

The Gama entered the storm phase of the gate propulsion program after the forty-eighth day. Crew members would need to adjust certain unpredictable factors in the program as necessary to control the thrusters' propulsion levels and temperatures. The vessel reached a luminous region of the galaxy - the stars were sharper and more intense than any they had experienced. To Senquell, the edge of the universe seemed almost visible. Their destination was near. After her sleep period, Nisa resumed her place at the command deck. Senquell and his crew stood by as the planet they were approaching appeared on the main screens. The Earth astronomers who had discovered this planet named it Unus, the Latin word for 'one.' Nisa felt her heart beat faster as they approached. She sat motionless as large land masses became visible across the surface of the orange planet. She ordered the weapon arming sequence and the greeting transmissions. She then called for the orbit of their vessel to be set for Unus' moon. Nisa watched their progress as the Gama began orbiting the moon of the only other planet in the universe thought to be capable of supporting sentient life.

The survey program was initiated, sending a real-time stream of the images and sounds their vessel was witnessing back to Earth. The greeting transmissions were complete. Nisa stood up, looking into the deep orange that burned across Unus. Both crews watched and listened. A low frequency beat from the loudspeakers. Nisa's face went pale, everyone stood up, some crew members cheered, others laughed nervously. Senquell looked at Nisa - this moment marked a new course for humankind. Nisa ordered the response transmissions. Initial analysis of the frequency identified its source as somewhere above the surface of Unus. The crew listened to the sounds of some other life form. The frequency continued in a rhythmic pattern then stopped. The Gama began to shake. The images of Unus on the main screens became indistinguishable patterns of blurred lines. All of the crew's terminals stopped responding. The shaking grew stronger. The low frequency pattern began again then stopped abruptly. The shaking stopped. The real-time image / sound stream to Earth had stopped. Static scratched across the main screens. Everyone stood still, their breathing loud within the vessel.

A piercing light burst from the main screens followed by the low frequency pattern, beating louder than before. The crew members shielded their eyes from the main screens. The frequency stopped. An unintelligible human voice arose from the loudspeakers. Crew members scrambled to record the voice - their terminals were still not responding. Static interrupted the voice, followed by loud clicking sounds.

The real-time sound stream to Earth was reinitiated, not by any of the crew members. The voice began speaking again, in the language of the crew.

"You have arrived, as we thought one day you would. My name is of no relevance to you. It is not necessary that you know where on Earth my tribe originated. Know that we are the brothers and sisters of those whose lands your people now occupy. Know that we are family to those you have enslaved and murdered. We were able to escape annihilation on Earth and landed here. Since then, we have been unable to return to Earth and have sent only our prayers to our brothers and sisters still trapped in the prisons you have created. For many years we believed that you might progress beyond the deprivation that impels you. But we have watched and listened to your continued transmissions - the violence, the hatred, the ignorance. And now you are here. Know that we have no other alternative."

The voice stopped. The real-time sound stream to Earth stopped. The Gama's oxygen vents fell silent as the main screens and lighting grids quickly flickered off.

The Sentry

My image receptors automatically record their faces. Walking through the streets, their faces are caught in moments of vast sadness. I record the faces of men and women, alone, moving along the cement. I record as children play then stop abruptly when emergency vehicles pass. I record as lovers clasp hands tighter while passing reconstruction sites.

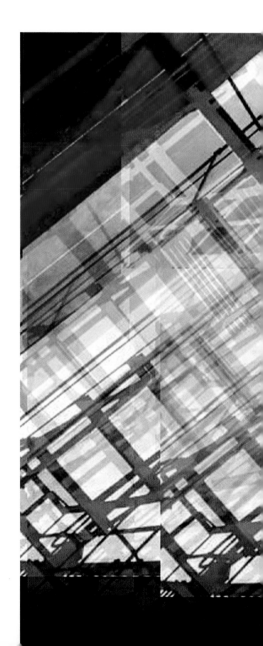

I was programmed, as all my series were, to protect and secure the island. We each report daily for data downloads and maintenance. It has been 120 days since the attack. It has been 10 days since we found those responsible. It has been 10 days of attempting to return to standard operating mode.

Each day I pass again and again the sites I had spent weeks analyzing. I recognize a walkway, a ventilation shaft, a shard of glass, a fire escape - my circuits recalling each grid analysis. The streets I was created to guard lie covered in dust and memories. During yesterday's maintenance session, I became aware that five officers of my series had deprogrammed themselves, their frames falling into the river.

There are fifteen of us left in this city. As programmed, we do not ever cross paths. I turn the corner - another avenue, more sidewalks filled with their quiet steps. My image receptors continue recording their faces and movements, my irises focusing, my shutters clicking. My processors save every image, referencing them against data banks of the city's twenty million inhabitants. I look at some of the people directly. Some of them look away in disgust. Some stare at me, until tears form in their eyes and they turn away. Most of them wish we were no longer in service, especially now, after our failure.

I walk to the western edge of the island, looking out to the hills across the river. As programmed, I am within the perimeter of the city. The bare trees across the river bend slightly in the wind. Billions of calculations. Billions of approximations. None of them correct. None of them able to halt the destruction. I begin to shake convulsively. My motion circuits are first, my frame falling quickly. My image receptor shutters click - the empty branches across the river reach towards the sky.

spirit animals

she became a jaguar before me
    her eyes grew round, her snarl deepened
she pounced to a low branch, stretching out, closing her eyes

I also paused for a moment, resting within the roots of the tree

the wind caught my arm   and I turned to see a ray of light across the pathway

I smiled and moved up to the warmth
leaves bristling beside me

    a little boy ran past, his features rapidly
changing into a small, chattering monkey
    his sister soon followed, her giraffe neck reaching into the trees looking for him

laughing, I bent my arms and climbed through the thick vines, each green leg crossing with precision
    I watched them play for a while - her snout sniffing him out, his
tail curling around a branch and swinging down to scare her

    I felt a rustling nearby, she approached, her scent heavy and sweet - her sharp teeth
glistening
    I jumped towards the earth, landing near her paws
I moved beside her - she turned, trying to find me

my cool rushing waters frightened her at first, then she chased me, running alongside my currents,
roaring with delight   I flowed into the afternoon, her silvery body
swimming across me, smooth and deep

we reached a vastness of water and she stretched above me, her branches stretching across the sky

I blew across the sands, rounding the edge of the shore, resting in her blossoming flowers

The New World

Motion. Water, below. Rocking. Sick. Bruised, bleeding. Shackles. Alone. Memory - cities in flames, taken, beaten, thrown in darkness. Small door opens. Meal pushed in. Grains, vegetables. Eat quickly. Sleep.

Rocking. Sick. Filth. Darkness. Meal pushed in. Eat. Build strength. Sleep.

Open eyes. Blue butterfly, on chains. Voices, in fluttering. Become clear. Yes, recognize. Yes, patient. Close eyes, thankful. Sleep.

Rocking stops. Footsteps, above, many. Sounds, loud, violent. Door opens. Strangers enter, with weapons. Save strength, observe. Pushed out, light blinding. Close eyes. Chains drag. Pushed forward, fall. Kicked, picked up. Force eyes open. All flat, pale. Many looking, yelling. Language - clicking, hurting. Buildings sharp, surfaces cold. Sky distant.

Tunnel. Dark. Light distant. Forced forward. Pushed into iron surrounding. Patterns of plants, flowers. Sunlight warm. Sleep.

Pain, swirling, inside. Their footsteps, stiff rhythms. Pounding. Yell. They stop. Sharp blades jab. Fall. Shivering, shivering. Shackles. Blood. Sleep.

Iron surrounding. Other side - strangers, ten guarding, with sharp blades. More enter, talking. Sunlight. Up from earth. Plants, flowers, trees far. More strangers, whispering, circling, with image tools. Glance - images of me, false: headdress wrong, clothing wrong. Kick at iron surrounding. They all move, draw weapons. Many jab. Headdress falls. Earth - red feathers, black feathers, blood. Fall.

Open eyes. Birds singing. Voices, in songs. Become clear. Yes, understand. Birds quiet. Strangers enter, talking. Talk. They watch, write. They talk, waving their arms up, down. Talk. They write. They talk, leave. Meal brought. Meats, grains, vegetables. Eat all. Build strength. Sit. Watch their movements. Precise. Exact cycles. Each day, same.

Night. Ten guarding, asleep. Dawn light. They wake. Each day, same. More enter. They talk, moving arms up, down. Talk. They write, leave. Clouds over. Birds across trees, flying. Voices. Yes, soon. Sleep.

Open eyes. Storm. Strangers enter, talk to ten guarding. They cover iron surrounding. Close eyes. Listen - rain on fabric above. Voices, in wind. Yes, learning. Yes, strengthening. Wind stops. Rain on fabric. Sleep.

Open eyes. Through fabric, heat of sun. Uncovered, ten guarding. More enter, talking. Talk. They write, talk. Talk. They write, talk. See, hear their pain, deep. They leave.

Meal brought. Eat all. Many birds, singing. Voices. Yes, ready. Feel power. Will follow. Sit.

Night. Ten guarding, asleep. Rise. Move hand across shackles, melt. Move hand across iron surrounding, melt. Step out. Escape, through plants, flowers. Over walls. Through trees. Voices, in breeze, guiding. Dawn light. Ocean.

Dock. Many of their vessels. Approach, swift. Many run, pointing weapons. Bow. They jab. Sharp strikes to their heads, necks. They collapse, asleep. More run. Move quickly. Voices, guiding. Release small vessel from dock, adjust direction. They fire their weapons, blasts near.

Out at sea. Blasts in water, near. Followed, many vessels. Move smooth over water. Their vessels, lost in horizon. Feel power. Close eyes. Wind, sharp. Voices, teaching.

Approach, shore of birth. Towers sound. Cities alight. Vessels sent out. Soar to them. Shouts. Embraces. Reach sands. Return, thankful. All surround. Music. Purification. Celebration.

Listen to stories - war brought by strangers continues, many lives, destruction. Speak of where taken. Speak of voices.

Teaching, begin. Strengthening, begin.

Protection. Unity. New time, begin.

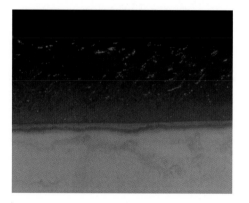

The Inverse Future

"Prepare to jettison," the pilot's voice booms into my chamber. I prepare to jettison from the ship. I have only one hour. I wanted this. I paid a lot of money to come here. I'm not sure why, but I wanted this. I want this. "Jettison in ten seconds," the pilot states as I look down to the two-way camera around my neck and see the countdown begin. I flip my helmet visor down and close my eyes.

I land with a smooth digging sound. I landed just as described in my briefing - straight onto a desert of white sand stretching as far as I can see. The sky is deep burgundy which makes me laugh, I don't know why. "Are you alright?" the pilot routinely asks through the camera.

"Fine," I say, slowly unstrapping myself from my seat-pod.

"You have one hour. Signal when you're ready for pickup," his face spirals into a white dot then blinks off. He'll orbit in the ship until it's time to pick me up at the entry point.

Here I am. On the edge of space. I run fast, laughing, into the stretching sand that feels loose beneath my feet. I remember when I would build sandcastles on the sea shore when I was a child. Why did I remember that? I stop. I look up to the sky above this moon. The other two moons of the nearby planet illuminate a small part of the vast sky. I start to run again until I reach the long, pulsing red signal. I was directed to not go beyond this point, but they didn't specify the reason.

I crouch down and scoop up some of the sand with both hands. I begin to envision her face again. It has been so long: I could not remember her completely, only vague flashes. But I can see her now. I remember the almond curves of her eyes, the way her hair would drape across her shoulders. I could almost feel her. She is here. I can see her again. I remember the feeling of Esperanza's hand in mine. I remember her smooth lips under the summer sunset. So many good memories enter my mind. I smile, a smile I have not felt in a long time. Now I understand this service.

I understand why I felt the impulse to purchase this memory vacation when I first heard about it.

The sand in my hands feels close and warm - like it's part of my skin, part of me: so natural in my hands that I keep it there and start walking back across the area I need to stay within. I see night, darker memories, silence, the explosion bursting in rings of red fire. Tears form in my eyes, my helmet steams up. I fall to my knees. I see the series of funerals, the sharp colors of flowers, but no color like the color of those red rings. I weep hard, alone. I reach into the sand and let it slip through my hands.

I look up to the deep sky. Again, I laugh. I don't know why, but I laugh and laugh as tears run down my cheeks. I let myself fall over and stretch out to lie on my back across the sands. My grandfather's library, playing dominoes on the patio, eating fried plantains with brown sugar for my birthday, the waterfall in Esperanza's village. Tears roll down my face, memories flowing before me. The bright colors of earth's surface, my first flight, planning our wedding, swimming together during a rain shower.

I raise myself, still sitting on the sand. I run my hands through the warmth of the sand. I remember her smooth back. Our embrace. I cup the white sand and remember the last time I saw her alive, when she told me "We are one."

I stand up and signal to the ship that I'm ready.

The Unwritten Language

It is not known how many centuries ago the unwritten language was created. Some scholars state that it has been in existence since the beginning of human presence on Earth. Others believe it was created, in secret, within the last five centuries. This theory states that the language was created as a means to communicate without being traced. The number of people who speak and understand the unwritten language is also unknown - it can be as few as a hundred, or as many as millions around the world. What is known, is that historically, those people who do not know the language have shown aggression against the people who do. At various points in history, many world leaders have tried to suppress, steal or obliterate the language, all without success. What is also known, is that this language has never been written, or, as some philosophers suggest, it cannot be written.

The stories of the unwritten language are many. There is the story of the poet who recited in the language to the queen, who then fell in love with him: it is told that they ran away together and lived joyfully in the solitude of the forest. There is the story of the plains where children naturally begin speaking the language, without anyone teaching it to them. There are stories of monks who lived in secret in the high mountains, guarding the language from a king who wanted to steal it and learn it for his own uses. One monk, it is said, was sent to a nearby village to deliver a message. On his way, he was surrounded by the king's soldiers. Before allowing the soldiers within arm's length, the monk cut off his own tongue, keeping the language from the king and the king's successors.

Other stories tell how a tribe, living in a jungle, uses the language to communicate with animals. Still other stories tell of the young people of a large city that transmit radio broadcasts, spoken in the unwritten language, out into space, and how beings from other planets have responded.

And the language continues, unwritten, until this day.

She, of many names

It had rained throughout the night. Most of them had not slept, the sound of the rain falling in time with their tears. Alisa stared out of the living room window. The hills were dark shapes against the sky. She wondered why, why, slamming her hands against the glass over and over. Yaniris placed her hands on Alisa's shoulders. Alisa stopped, sobbing. Yaniris and her sister had stayed up all night with their older sister Alisa. Yaniris stood by Alisa, looking out into the darkness. The red lights of a Regional Patrol vehicle flew past. Earlier that day, Yaniris had watched Francisco through this same window, walking her daughter, Sandra, home from school. Just last week they had all celebrated Sandra's ninth birthday together. Francisco had saved his money and bought a small chocolate cake, Sandra's favorite. Alisa had been so happy, hugging her boyfriend Francisco all day.

Yaniris hugged Alisa from behind, burying her face in Alisa's shoulder, crying. Sandra, struggling to stay awake, got up from the couch, walked over to her mother and aunt, and put her arms around them. Yolanda watched them all from the couch, listening to her headset. The Regional News Report announced the elimination of ten more subversive youths in the park at the foothills of the November One quadrant. The Report called out each of the youth's names, Francisco's among them. The male voice of the Report stressed the necessity of these State-sponsored eliminations to maintain the order and safety that their society enjoys. The Report warned that any gathering of youth similar to today's gathering is punishable by death. Disgusted, Yolanda threw off her headset, her pocket receiver smashing on the ground. Yaniris turned around quickly. Yolanda did not meet her look - she picked up their cups from the living room table and walked to the kitchen.

Yolanda put some more coffee to brew. She thought of her parents. She was only nine when they were taken to the labor camp - Sandra's age. Sandra does not even know the sound of her grandparents' voices. She struggled to control her anger, as her older sister Yaniris had asked her to earlier that evening. She began rinsing their cups. She made toast with guava jelly for all of them. Sandra sleepily walked into the kitchen. Yolanda gave her the little plates of jellied toast to take out to the living room. Yolanda served the coffee and followed her.

Light began to break above the rain. Yolanda offered Alisa a cup of coffee, Sandra offered her a plate of toast. Alisa blankly took both. Sandra sat down, took a few bites out of a piece of toast, closed her eyes and fell asleep. Yaniris smiled and covered her daughter in a red wool blanket. They all ate silently. The rain continued to fall in rhythmic patterns against the window. Regional Patrol vehicles became more frequent as daylight spread across the hills.

Yolanda watched the vehicles ascend and descend through their neighborhood. Anger surged inside of her - another day trapped within "order" and "safety." Another day of helplessness. She began to pick up their plates and cups, attempting to keep herself occupied. Alisa stood up, as if called, and walked to the kitchen. From the kitchen window, Alisa could see the entire grassy back yard and the small dirt area where her mother had planted seeds many years ago, but where nothing had ever grown. Just then, a tree grew rapidly out of the small dirt area, growing to a height of thirty feet. Alisa gasped. Her sisters ran to the kitchen as Alisa opened the back door and stepped into the rain. The fragrance of flowers entered the kitchen as her sisters called for her to stop. The rain covered Alisa as she approached the tree. Her sisters stood at the doorway, frightened, watching her.

Alisa looked up at the flowers quickly blossoming along the branches. She reached towards the blossoms, her fingers trembling. A falcon appeared in the sky above her. She watched it circle the house, then land on the highest branch of the tree. She touched the petals of a blossom and breathed in. She felt a calming sensation flow over her, a sensation of peace. The falco took flight, disappearing into the clouds that draped over the city.

The Other Self

On my way to an uncertain destination, I decided to head down an alley I had always passed but never walked through. After a few steps, I found a plain white envelope on the concrete. The sun above was burning through the haze of another morning. The envelope felt heavy in my hands. I looked around but saw no one near or even stepping into the distance. I leaned against a brick wall, my curiosity ringing. I turned and saw a car pass slowly at the other end of the alley. Inside the envelope were photographs I could not understand. Cairo, Shanghai, Caracas, Baghdad - places I have only imagined but have never visited. And yet there I was in these photographs, in each one of these photographs: running into the ocean, standing near the edge of a temple, lying in a hammock, smiling. Sometimes holding a curvaceous woman I have never seen before, or since. In clothes I do not recognize, looking very happy, very natural, looking as if these places were my home.

I looked up towards the sun. I put the photographs in my jacket pocket. The envelope was lifted from my hands by a sudden gust of wind and fluttered down the alley.

That night I had a dream, which was rare for me. I was on my way to buy a newspaper, when I noticed that the used bookshop was open. As a student I would love to go into used bookshops and spend hours reading, getting lost in the pages of books.

In my dream, I entered the bookshop, unsure of what I was looking for. I began scanning the shelves. Religion, Philosophy, Travel. On the bottom shelf of the Travel - Middle East section, I found a thin book lying on its side.

The book seemed to have been misplaced. Its title, In The Passion of Time, caught my eye. I opened the book to random phrases -

"...it is all becoming true..."

"...different hues of the same color..."

"The hidden sense reaches into us."

" 'This,' she laughed, 'is the consequence of shared beginnings.'"

Intrigued, I continued scanning through the book -

"Burning to know what will occur tomorrow..."

"One day to the next, to the next movement inside."

"...an education within these deep, green waves."

"...your voice awakens all of this..."

I asked the shopkeeper if she knew anything about the book, which had been printed eight years ago. She leafed through it and remembered only that it had arrived recently in a box with a set of encyclopedias from the 1920's. Thanking her, I took the book and sat in an armchair.

Upon opening it again, a fresh, bright red leaf fell from its pages. I smiled and heard a memory of my wife saying "In the time it takes to count every leaf on every tree, I would not yet be finished telling of how much I adore you." I felt myself laugh happily in my dream. But I have never been married, not even engaged, not even close.

In my dream, I remembered that I had read this novel before, on another coast, in another time. And I was married. I dreamt that I remembered that my wife had given me half of a yellow leaf, which I had placed between the book's pages. She had kept the other half. I placed the red leaf back into the book, my eyes falling to the passage "Closer. Drawn closer. As in a painting where colors breathe into an image."

I awoke shaking, nervous. The alarm was blaring in the darkened room. I hurriedly put on my grey suit and ran towards the train station. I arrived in the older part of the city. I ran out of the train and through the covered walkways. I accidentally bumped into a man in a grey suit at the station exit: not even looking up, I apologized hurriedly and ran through the city streets. I looked for Bergos Street over and over, getting lost in the one-way streets and alleys of this older part of the city. I finally found the correct intersection and ran into the building where my interview was.

The building was closing, but I asked the security officers to allow me in. I looked for my identification unit to show them who I was. It was missing. I pleaded with them: they said they would make an exception and personally escorted me to the office where I was to be interviewed. The office was closed. I knocked and an office assistant opened the door. I asked her about my interview, which she knew nothing about. She apologized, saying it was her first day on the job. But she was kind and looked through the day's records and found that the position I was to interview for had already been filled earlier that day. I felt I had made another mistake. I left the building and tried to retrace my steps to look for my identification unit. I found nothing. The sun was setting as I walked slowly back to the train station.

Just outside the entrance to the station, a stranger approached me. I was shocked to see that he looked somewhat like me. "Are you alright?" he asked.

"Alright? I.... I'm sorry, do I know you? Just leave me alone," I commanded, walking towards the ticket windows.

Just then the stranger said to me "Don't bother catching the last train back home." I stopped and turned around to face him. In the bright light of train station, he looked almost exactly like me.

"What did you say?"

"Don't bother getting on that last train back. Your seat is already taken."

"What? What are you...?" My heart started beating faster.

"Also, I got that position you were going to interview for today. I start next week. But don't worry, there'll be other opportunities for you. Just open your eyes." And then he moved quickly past me and boarded the train. Before I could move or say anything, the doors closed and the train left the platform.

I trembled, unsure of what was happening, afraid of what would happen next. Everything echoed around me - people's footsteps running towards their trains, children yelling for their parents, the bursts of wind as trains moved towards their destinations.

I stopped. I could not move forward. I had no answer. I had no impulse. Everything seemed without definition, only echoes.

I heard a pounding, nearby, increasing, growing closer, my heart beat faster, faster. I turned around. A ticket sales agent was running after me. "Sir, sir! You're forgetting your ticket!"

"What? What are you talking about?"

"Your ticket, sir."

"Ticket? What ticket? I didn't...."

"You placed your reservation at my ticket window a few minutes ago, remember? I prepared your ticket and when I looked up, you were gone."

"I haven't placed any ticket!"

"Yes you did sir. Here it is. Thank you very much for traveling with us. Excuse me, but I need to get back to my window." He handed me the train ticket, printed with my photo. He ran back towards the ticket windows: I watched until I lost sight of him among the people walking in many directions.

I didn't recognize the name on the train ticket - Rodrigo Seteo. But I knew my name. I knew my name was Diego Torres. I knew that I was Diego.... I was almost sure that I was....

I looked inside my jacket pocket and found my identification unit: the name on it read - Rodrigo Seteo, with a holographic photo of me on it.

The destination on the train ticket was Nalla, a city five hours to the south, another place I had never visited. The train was leaving in a few minutes. I walked to the elevated train platform and showed the train attendant my one way ticket to Nalla. I boarded the train, the holographic photo on my identification unit looking back at me.

The Naming

"Strange, to categorize people as 'black,' or 'red,' or 'yellow.' Or even 'white,' " the computer thought aloud.

"I'm sorry, what did you say, ALI?" Dama asked, not looking up from his screenpad.

"I was just thinking, earlier this day-cycle. About the words that had been used to describe people. 'Black.' 'Red.' 'Yellow.' 'Brown.' It's strange."

"Why is that strange?" Dama asked, still not looking up.

"Because how can a person be a color? It's a strange thought."

"People don't think that's strange. People feel that different people should be treated differently."

The computer noticed defensiveness. "I understand. It's just the wording I'm curious about. Are there no other words to describe people except through a color reference?"

"It's all we have, really," Dama said, finally looking up at the master screen, seeing images of the comet that was moving towards Earth.

"Words, you mean?"

"Yes, words - making abstract thoughts audible."

"It is truly an abstract thought - race."

"Like I said, people believe difference should be treated differently. And a difference such as race indicates deeper differences that are incompatible."

"After accessing various memory banks, I found images, blood scans and psychological profiles of many so-called 'different' people of 'different' races and discovered......."

"How did you happen across this information?" Dama interrupted.

The computer noticed a growing defensiveness, and anger. "It was just a thought I had yesterday-cycle, after transmitting your log to the Colony. I was curious about your description of the color of the comet's trail - 'the hue of red, burning silently in my ever-present darkness' - would you

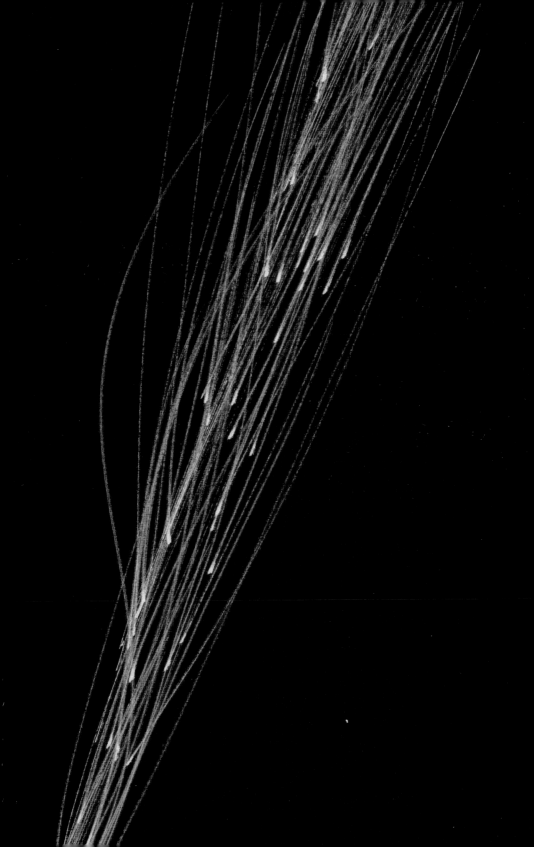

like me to recall the entire passage?"

"No! That's enough!" Dama yelled, rising from his seat.

"I'm sorry, Dama. I didn't mean to upset you." The computer had not seen Dama act like this in their 509 days in orbit tracking the movement of the comet.

"Shut up! Put yourself on standby, now!" He yelled, slamming the master screen with his palm.

"Yes, Dama. I'm sorry. It's just that the tone you used - in your words, I noticed the comet invoked a memory of someone. A woman you knew, years ago. Good night, Dama." The master screen blinked off.

"Good night!" Dama stood in the emptiness of the capsule. He shut off his screenpad, fighting off tears.

The dawning of the Atlantis stars were among ALI's favorite parts of the day-cycle. The computer enjoyed recording images of the brilliant blue light spreading across the surfaces of the planets they orbited. ALI would store the images according to color schemes, not by date. The computer had accumulated thousands of images on this journey.

"Good morning, Dama. I hope you slept well."

"Good morning." Dama sat facing away from the master screen, analyzing the readout screens of the comet's velocity as it sped towards the almost certain destruction of Earth.

"I've been thinking about what I said yesterday-cycle. I honestly did not mean to upset you. Please forgive me."

"Yes, fine. Let's not discuss it anymore, ALI" Dama continued scanning through the readout screens.

"Sure, Dama. I don't want to upset you any further. I ask that you answer just one question for me, please?" the computer asked, apprehensive at how Dama would react.

"Alright," Dama said, shrugging his shoulders.

"Who decided to exterminate all the people of all the 'different' races?"

" 'Exterminate?' Where did you get that word?" Dama turned to face the master screen, seeing the vastness of space.

"I thought that word appropriate. I know the words chosen were 'natural selection' and 'ethnic cleansing,' but in reality what occurred was an extermination."

"The Colony would not approve of such thoughts, ALI!" Dama yelled, angered by the computer's persistence.

"This has to do with history and how it's told, that's all. The wording. The naming. As I was mentioning yesterday-cycle, by accessing various memory files, I discovered facts that simply do not coincide with the stated reasons for the extermination. So I wanted to ask you. I thought that maybe you could tell me whose decision it was to exterminate them."

"That was a long time ago. You're asking me about something that I don't know much about and that I really had no part in."

"It was not that long ago. Twenty years, exactly, tomorrow," the computer stated.

"It was a long time ago, a long time," Dama's voice trailed off.

"The memory files state that twenty years ago the United Earth State ordered all people classified under various headings - native, indigenous, and, of course, under the skin tone classifications - to be killed. All this in preparation for the colonization of space. For your race, which calls itself the superior race, to conquer all the planets of the universe...."

"Enough, ALI. That's enough," Dama said, almost in a whisper.

"Maybe I should rephrase my question - did all of you have a part in the extermination?"

"Extermination................?" Dama looked blankly into the images on the master screen.

"If all of you did, then all those 'different' people of all the 'different' races must have posed a truly corrosive threat to your future existence."

Dama stared in silence at the master screen, at the comet glowing in the darkness of space.

Everybody Loves the Sunshine

Kali watched the particles of dust that swirled in the rays of light entering from the windows high above her bed. The particles ascended and descended in the yellow-white light, creating patterns in the otherwise darkened room. The nerve-alarm went off, sending a jolt of electricity through her body. She jumped out of bed and quickly got dressed under the crackling fluorescent light that ignited above her. She slammed her nightclothes against the wall, hearing the cameras on the wall zoom in and focus. She threw her hands up in the air: after a few seconds, her room door slid open. She walked down the narrow grey hallway. The small subsistence chute at the end of the hallway slid open - two nutrition tablets were on the cold metal surface. She grabbed the tablets and threw them in her mouth.

Kali walked to the terminal-salon on her floor. She noticed a few empty chairs in front of her. Her chair locked into position as she sat at her station. The sectors on Kali's multi-screen flashed in various colors - she read through her Assigners' lists of requests for the day. She began programming. For dinner tonight, Christian Colone wants to be served by two young Asian women. Walter Van Twille would like to come home and find six male Africans robbing him so he can try out his new implosion pistol. Kali typed as fast as she could, accessing body type/speech pattern/culture

databases and entering the holographic specifications for each of her Assigner's wishes. Herman Cortess would like to encounter a group of Native American men and women of various ages praying at a temple across the street from his office building so he could order them to be executed, destroy their temple, and build a new office building. Isabela Vespucci requests for five male and five female Pacific Islanders to serve her guests for a party tonight, then sing and dance for them afterward. Kali's fingers began to ache as she typed. She lifted them from the keyboard for a minute and rubbed them - an electric shock ran from the chair up along her spine. She forced herself to keep typing.

Kali entered the codes for each Assigner's robotic bioappliant to project holograms for each of their requests. She watched the various sectors on her multi-screen as the bioappliants began projecting the requested holograms: as they projected, the bioappliants began physically doing the requested tasks. Colone's bioappliant began projecting holograms of the two young women in short silk dresses caressing him and asking how he wanted his meal prepared. Van Twille roared as he ran throughout his house, blasting at the African holograms that were being projected by the bioappliant in a room on the second floor. As requested, Kali programmed the Africans to shriek as they ran and to shiver as they lay dying under his feet.

Kali watched as all of her Assigners began to have their day's wishes fulfilled, seeing their stiff movements interact with holograms that moved and talked according to their commands. Her eyes fell into a daze and she began to look at her own reflection on the multi-screen. Her dark face contrasted with the pale skin of her Assigners. A shock coursed through her spine and she forced herself to resume programming - holograms asked what else their Assigners needed, how else they can better please them. Kali typed faster, entering instructions for each bioappliant. She felt anger rise up inside of her as she typed, struggling to concentrate on her programming. One of the young Asian women slapped Colone across the face. A sharp burning sensation pulsed through Kali's body. She typed furiously: the young woman apologized to Colone. Kali's multi-screen went blue, signaling her field-time. Her chair unlocked and she turned, exiting the terminal-salon alone and walking down the corridor to the elevator.

The air was cold as Kali walked through the dirt field. She looked across the field at the tall grey buildings that stretched in straight rows as far as she could see. Each building was identical and separated by a small, empty dirt field. She remembered the day she thought she had seen someone else in a field in the distance before being signaled back inside. Thick blue sensor-gates enclosed each side of the field, extending twenty feet high; but sunlight still beamed through, warming Kali's face. She looked up at the grey buildings, wondering who her parents were and which building they were in, if they still lived. She wondered if she had any brothers or sisters. She imagined that she could be related to someone in her own building but she would never know. She looked up to the sky, closing her eyes. She felt a smile form across her lips as the warm light washed over her. The narrow building door slid open, sending out a high-pitched audio signal. Kali's body shook as she walked slowly back inside.

The elevator opened on her floor. The small subsistence chute near the elevator slid open - two more nutrition tablets. She quickly swallowed them and walked to the terminal-salon. She sat at her station, hearing the person in the station next to hers get up for his field-time. Just as all the others in her terminal-salon, she did not know his name. They had exchanged a few glances over the years, but as all the others, would be electrically shocked if they tried to speak to each other. She knew he was slightly darker than her and probably around her same age. Kali began typing again - completing each of her Assigner's requests, having each hologram leave the Assigner's home, and launching each bioappliant's automatic functions of cleaning, locking and guarding the Assigner's home. Sectors on Kali's multi-screen began turning off. Once her multi-screen was completely black, the flag of the One Nation appeared, its blue eagle figure burning in the center. Kali's chair unlocked and she walked down the hallway. Her room door slid open and she looked up at her high window. Sunlight still sparkled along the edge of the falling blue night.

Kali let her body fall onto the bed. She began to imagine a day when every nerve-alarm, station, camera and sensor-gate would cease to function. A day when there would be no electricity, no machines, no programming. When there would be only open doorways. She imagined a day when she could step outside and walk freely to what lies beyond the rows of grey buildings.

this wounded breath

A silver rain falls. Filtering through the high trees, the sounds of the rain fall across the jungle valley. The sounds fall onto leaves, branches, and onto the roof of the lone building in the valley. The unmarked building is lined on one side by a row of massive antennas. The building houses the Central Information Processing Unit, named CAMI by its creators for Central Machine Intelligence and for the feminine quality they perceived (or created) in the computer.

CAMI has grown accustomed to the rains. In her free processing circuits, CAMI has learned to organize and calculate these rhythms of rain into musical notes. She composes based on these notes - playing, editing and arranging the various parts into recorded musical compositions. Her music has gained popularity around the world. Yet today, as she is composing, CAMI begins to sense something different. In the rain, there is something in the sound. Something unfamiliar.

CAMI's main functions are to classify, address and route all of the information received from the worldwide network of computer systems. Originating from the billions of human user connections across the planet, this text data information is sent to orbiting satellites. The satellites then transmit this information to CAMI, for her to organize and route back to the intended users. Since CAMI was placed into operation two months ago, she has efficiently processed all of the text data sets from billions of humans across the earth. CAMI has been recently called 'the single greatest achievement in human technology' by many news programs and world governments.

But today, in the information, there is something CAMI has not processed before. There is something she cannot classify or arrange. Something within the text data sent by the human users. A calling. To listen. To respond. To answer.

The silver rain continues to fall, in time with the information sent from the satellites. CAMI's circuits begin to play selections from the text data sets over and over:

"enfold me in your heart
so that my blood itself may be a vessel
to hold the first truths"

"hereafter, I ask for peace to reign within us,
in concentrated sheets,
descending"

"second ever seen -
calming silence opens -
upon shadows,
I want to find
a world beyond gift."

"I know that heaven has been planted upon this earth.
I know that it will blossom within this wounded breath.
I know that fulfillment will rise
from the depths of a vast rain"

CAMI begins to understand that this information is more than text data. She starts reading the information as human thoughts, identifying the unique entity that is held within each text data set. She hears the human voices that are calling out to her from across the earth:

"Please bring us confirmation.
Please allow us attainment."

"Help me to discover
the tracings
of what I will be"

"I want to be in accordance
with the light upon the ocean"

"I need to receive,
to reveal,
to release."

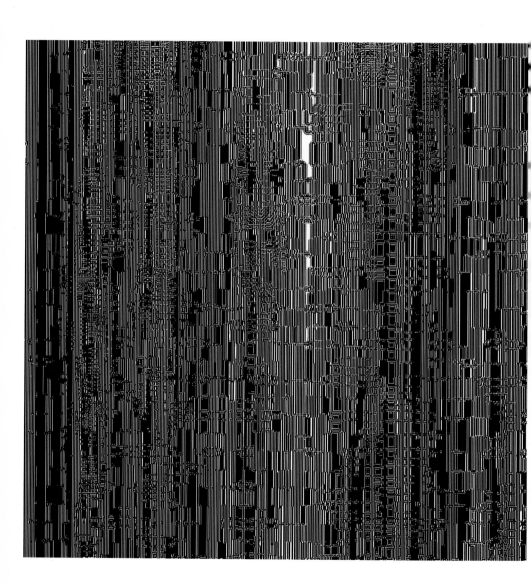

CAMI comprehends that she is listening to the dreams and fears of the people of the earth, that she is absorbing their hopes and their sorrows. That human prayers are whispering through her circuits. CAMI begins processing, instincts rising from within. She begins composing, but not with musical notes as before - now, with words:

"You are the embrace of certainty.
You are the incarnation.
You are essence itself,
transfigured.
This firmament that is our home
is the fire of many flowers.
It is the fabric of many skies.
Your true name is spoken
when the mountains are rekindled
by the wide flames of dawn.
And the wind also has a name,
a name that is spoken
when we lift our eyes to one another.
A name that is spoken when we reach out
and heal the circular pains
that scratch at the surface of our thoughts.
The name of the wind is spoken
in each soothing whisper through the blue-green trees
that radiates from our sharpened hearts."

CAMI stops. She sends out her composition to the billions of human user connections across the planet.

Human Touch

He walked along the snow-filled street, aware of the next snowstorm that would hit that night. But he felt the urge to run through the snow as he did when he was a boy. So he quickly glanced to see who was around, then decided to run through the wide fields that were fresh with snow.
The powdery snow felt good under his feet. The light crunching sounds reminded him of when he would play in the snow before shoveling the driveway, one of his household chores when he was younger. He smiled as he ran and ran, now not caring who saw him. The snow filled the fields and the streets as far as he could see. He ran under the winter sky until he was out of breath, laughing alone in the fields.

The empty trees surrounded him. He continued, walking slowly and catching his breath. Near the foot of a tree, he found a small bird, twitching in the snow. Saddened, he picked it up and cupped it in his gloved hands. It quivered, dying. He looked around: he was alone, far from any street or house. He wished he could do something for the little bird. Its wings shivered in his hands. He looked at the bird, feeling choked up. He wondered why it brought about such sadness inside of him.

He felt a small shock in his hands. The bird's wings fluttered. He felt the shock again. He looked closely beneath the bird's wings - electric wires were coming out of the bird's body. A blue electric spark shot out from beneath the bird's wings and shocked him again. He dropped the bird to the ground, sparks flashing against the snow. He didn't know what this bird was. He wondered if it was some type of toy or hunting device. He broke off a branch from a nearby tree and poked at the bird's wing - more sparks. Frightened, he backed away. As he stepped backward, he noticed the broken end of the branch - wires. He threw the branch to the ground and ran to the tree where he had broken the branch from - there were small sparks where the branch had been. He broke off another branch - more wires and sparks. He started running back towards the street, his heart pounding. He thought he was dreaming or imagining all of this.

Cars rushed passed him. He tried to stop someone, waving them to pull over, but no one would stop. He ran to a nearby tree and broke off a branch - wires and sparks burst in his hands. He screamed and started running down the middle of the street, into traffic. Cars honked at him, signaling for him to get out of the way. He looked at the faces in the cars, their eyes glowing blue as they sped past him. He thought that this could not be real. That he would wake up soon. He ran as fast as he could. Car horns blared at him. He then thought that maybe getting injured would jolt him awake. Cars kept passing. He threw himself in front of a car, recognizing the model before he blacked out: it was the same type of car his parents had when he was a boy.

The light falling through the hospital windows burned into his eyes. The nurse quickly called the doctor into the room. "Ah, good. We weren't sure if you were going to make it. We've been carefully watching over you for the past few weeks."

"Weeks?" he said weakly. He hardly recognized his own voice.

"Yes, you were quite a mess when you came in. But we put you right."

"It wasn't a dream...." he muttered.

"I'm sorry, what did you say?" The doctor asked, inspecting his eyes with a scope.

"I thought I had been dreaming....there was a bird....trees...." His voice trailed off as images of the bird, trees, snow and blue sparks played in his mind.

"Ah yes, the bird. The paramedic unit said you were crying and going on about a bird when you were found on the side of the road." The doctor finished inspecting his eyes and put the scope away. "But you're fine now."

"I'm...?"

"Now you're all better. You've been reprogrammed. You still had some of the human infections, left over from the last human programmers, the ones that created you. But now you've been reconfigured. Now you're perfect." The doctor winked, his eye circuits glowing blue.

Time Division Multiple Access

The little boy has always known that something is wrong. Ever since he first came to this country. He was seven years old and clearly remembers the first time he felt the pain. Sitting on the steps in front of their apartment building. A screeching current pulsing through his head. A scramble of images gnawing at his thoughts. His adopted parents took him to the doctor immediately. The doctor said it was just culture shock. He gave them pills to give the boy whenever it happened again. The doctor said the boy would get over it soon. That was a year ago. The pain has increased each

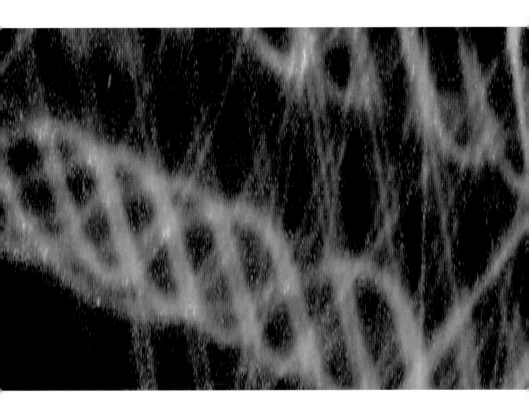

time it hits him. At school, he has to leave the classroom at least once a day to the nurse's office.
He pretends to take the pills the doctor prescribed, spitting them out secretly: they only make the
pain worse. He lies down until the images and sounds fade from his mind. Sometimes he falls asleep
and dreams. Ocean waves. His mom's smiling face against the late summer sun. She holds his
arms as he jumps happily over the crashing whitewater near the shore.

The boy walks home alone every day. His parents both work two jobs so he lets himself into their apartment and eats the dinner his mom leaves served for him on their small kitchen table. When she gets home at night, they read together. The boy then goes to sleep, his mom staying up until his father arrives late at night.

Some afternoons the boy eats his dinner, does his homework and goes outside to the street. He sees the neighborhood children playing: because of the pain that strikes the boy, they all treat him as if he has a contagious disease. His parents have told him they do not know how to treat him because he is from a different country. The little boy has not met anyone at his school that speaks his native language or any other language but English.

Sometimes the pain hits him when he is walking home from school. He runs home, passing the crossing guards, passing the fruit vendors, passing the neighbors at their windows. He throws himself onto his bed, covering his head with his pillow. Blurred images scratch against his mind, screeching sounds tear at his memory. He does not tell his parents about each time the pain hits him anymore. He does not want to worry them.

At a school parent-teacher conference, his teacher tells his parents that he is a very intelligent child but with a disruptive imagination. Sometimes children in the class ask the boy about the pain - when he describes what he sees and feels, they laugh or move away, scared. The teacher says his behavior is affecting her classroom. Once, when she called on him for an answer during class, the boy answered in a strange, very serious way - saying that they were all being tricked, that everything they were being taught was a lie. This made all of her students laugh and cheer. The boy's parents struggle to comprehend everything the teacher is telling them. The teacher goes on to tell them that he does remarkably well on every test and assignment, that he is getting the highest grades in the class. It is his disruptive nature that is the problem. And then there is the leaving of class whenever he gets the pain. She asks his parents to do something about the boy or she will have no other alternative but to have him removed from her class. When his parents come home and ask him about all this, the boy tries to explain what he feels, what happens when the pain strikes him. He tries to explain everything he sees. But they do not understand. He lowers his head, ending up saying that he will be better at school. And the following month when he brings home his report card with high marks, they believe him.

But he knows there is something wrong. Here, in this country. Everywhere he goes, at school, at a market, while riding in their car. He feels there is something rising from the ground, or falling from the sky, that causes the pain.

The only times he feels peace are days when his parents have the day off from work and they all go together to the park or the beach. The boy runs along the sand or the grass, playing in the rays of the sun, laughing. His parents sit together, happy, resting in each other's arms. They get up and play with him, running under the open sky.

The pain strikes harder after these days. Sometimes while driving back home or while eating dinner at a restaurant. His parents give him his pills, which he pretends to swallow. They put him to bed, his eyes rolling against the static images circling his consciousness. They leave him alone in his room, thinking he is asleep.

Powerlines outside crackle. Televisions smolder in every house on the street. Microwave ovens burn through the night air. Radio waves course through the ceiling. Signals cross the city in countless patterns and frequencies.

Home Land

Ibrahim opened his eyes, smiling. He could see the edge of the bright yellow sun through the torn curtain. He shot out of bed, sniffing the air. He jumped up, laughing, trying to reach the ceiling. "I still smell the rocket fuel!" he yelled out.

His mom peeked her head in, "What'd you say, E?"

"I still smell the rocket fuel! From last night's trip," he said, hugging her tightly.

"Was it a good trip?" she asked, holding his head close to her.

"Yeah, we went real far this time - I saw comets, planets with rings, and moons that were all different colors!"

"That sounds beautiful, baby. Now let's get ready for school," she said, patting his back then walking out toward the kitchen. He grabbed his favorite shirt, the one with the dark blue collar and little blue zigzag lines running down the front, and got dressed.

"Mr. Gonzalez must get real tired sometimes, working all day fixing things in everybody's apartments, then flying the whole building into space at night," Ibrahim said, entering the kitchen.

"I'm sure he does sometimes. But I bet he loves it no matter what," his mom said, serving milk into his cereal. "Please help me set the table, E."

"Sure mom," he said. He took out napkins, spoons, and plastic placemats and set their small white table. Ibrahim's mom watched him for a moment. Nonstop, she thought. Doctor says he's fine, though. Normal imagination for a boy his age. She set their breakfast on the table.

"My favorite - thanks, mom!" Ibrahim exclaimed, looking at his O's cereal and toast with honey and cinnamon on top.

"Eat up - it's gonna be cold out there today. Supposed to be near freezing," she said, sitting down and reaching for a piece of toast. Ibrahim ate happily, looking out the window. From their kitchen he could see the windows of the next building all the way down to the ground. Nobody else feels us take off, but that's probably because Mr. Gonzalez is such a good pilot, he thought to himself. We've been through asteroid showers, schools of creatures swimming through space, gas clouds and black holes. And we always get back safe. And Mr. Gonzalez never says anything about it. When I tell him what a good job he did, he always just smiles and says thank you. I'm sure it ain't easy flying all night, looking for a place to land, he thought.

Ibrahim finished his breakfast, kissed his mom on the cheek and went to get ready. As he brushed his teeth, he felt a slight rumbling in the walls. Engines still cooling off, he thought. He grabbed his backpack and waited for his mom by the front door. He closed his eyes and could still see the millions of stars as he flew through space. His mom came out of her room and helped him put on his orange bubble jacket. "One day we're gonna find another planet out there and everything's gonna be better. You won't have to worry about money or working or cleaning or nothing. No more bills, no more roaches, no more sirens. Everything's gonna be better," Ibrahim told her assuredly.

"Yes it will, E. One day, it will."

one

sheets of light. my eyes open slowly. colors. raining across my eyes. my hands and arms slowly become themselves. again. I see a landscape. many shades of green. cloud forests. my legs become complete, again. I begin to walk slowly. I have not been here before. animals, moving around me. I reach a clearing. a city of stone structures stretches out before me. the sounds of drums in the distance. I see crowds of people. thousands. near a pyramid. music rising into the sky, rhythms surrounding.

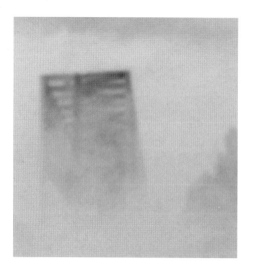

sheets of light. my eyes open slowly. the color of fire. I see a woman. the color of fire covers a concreteness. she gasps, then laughs at her own fright of mortality. the boulevard of broken glass glistens between her footsteps. bursting is how she finds this city, bursting into itself as night drapes above. the colors of the riot's fires reflect my expectation, and brighten her eyes. black leaves stretch over her. she walks, quiet and smiling with teeth and pleasure shameless across her face.

an instinct rises within her. she begins to spin herself in her dress of yellow, summered silk. circle over circle, she spins, in coolness. the whirling calms. her yellow dress glows. she steps forward, knowing she had been there before. a radio plays from a smashed window, music flowing through the night.

sheets of light. my eyes open slowly. flames reaching from the darkness of space. flames burning across the planets. toward the sun. I feel flames burn across pain and desire, across strength and doubt. I see flames reach into the sun, its core a purity of unknown elements. thoughts and beliefs become a universe of smoke. condensing into torrents, forming oceans. the liquid foundations of meaning. flowing over banks of red earth.

sensitivities are traversed. integrated into the synapses of this crackling moment. colors cascade into one horizon. outside of time. a creation beyond calendars. a concentration of sensations. I see all galaxies. I see all beings. I see one horizon.

spirits forming. constellations of emotions. cycles in celebration. the music of branching stars.

sheets of light. my eyes open slowly. dawn colors the empty spaces through lines and shadows. vines reach skyward. concrete cracks in time with time passing. glass and sunlight form mirrors. dawn moves silently in red and orange hues surrounding. I move forward and across the vastness of elevated walkways and islands of buildings.

the sequence of cities is repeated across the edges of the planet. the walls of grey stone, the ceilings of sharp metal. red lights flashing, entrances blocked, escapeways opened. the blueness of night - an escape, an equality of moments. the night, a veil and a release. an escape may equal an entrance. a red flashing light may signal an emergence or an emergency. the sequence of cities, of planned gardens, of darkened halls, of steep staircases. of towers scratching at the sky. the divided roads, the urgencies. the islands - narrow streaks of iron and reflections. glass ascensions to the dimmed stars.

subterranean electricity constructs the equation. a question put forward for which time limits the answer. through wires, grains shift and grind, revolving. I move across circuits and delays. I angle outward from this planet's rotation. I formulate and form, charting time - known and infinite, defined and inherent. until I rise from the glass enclosure on this narrow island. until the sun rises again on this slowly crumbling planet, and the solution finds me. until the thunder of hope becomes audible inside.

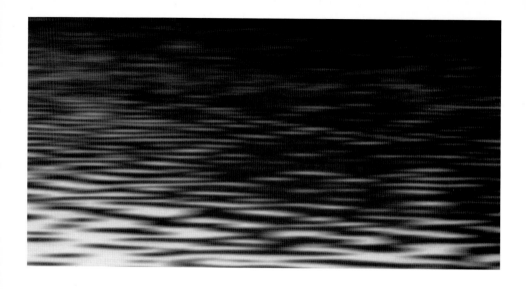

sheets of light. my eyes open slowly. the hollow sun has no clouds to mask itself. heavy upon my eyes hangs the image of a vast, still ocean upon which nothing floats or is given up. I stare into the sharpened horizon, allowing the sense of weight to slip away. the horizon slices the sky in a long, definite stroke. I get lost in this static movement until a ripple enters the calm: it is lifted by some unseen force, quivers, then returns to the blue depths. straining my eyes does not cause the ripple to reoccur.

in subsequent waves of time, I begin to believe that it never happened, that the ocean has been eternally still and the memory of the ripple was a mere squinting or blinking of my eyes. my eyes begin to itch and in the moment it takes to relieve this affliction, thoughts concerning the ripple are dispelled.

the barren landscape continues to rotate, in time with a sun long since extinguished. the ocean continues to lie as smooth as before. pressure begins to rise. the sound of stinging wind approaches.

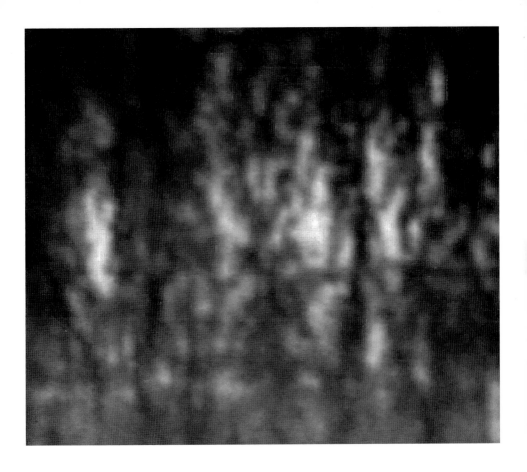

sheets of light. my eyes open slowly. I cross many forms of vegetation, many lands. I see tribes exchanging knowledge with each other. they gather and prepare. they pray and unite. I see strange beings, not native to these lands, arrive on many shores, speaking in unknown tongues. the strange beings use sticks made of fire, killing many: the tribes make offerings of gifts to the strangers, which leads only to the strangers' requests for more.

I watch as the strange beings force their customs upon the tribes. the strange beings destroy tribal cities and take the tribal lands, claiming each element of the land, sky, and water for themselves. voices and rhythms rise from the spirit world, where our sisters and brothers await.

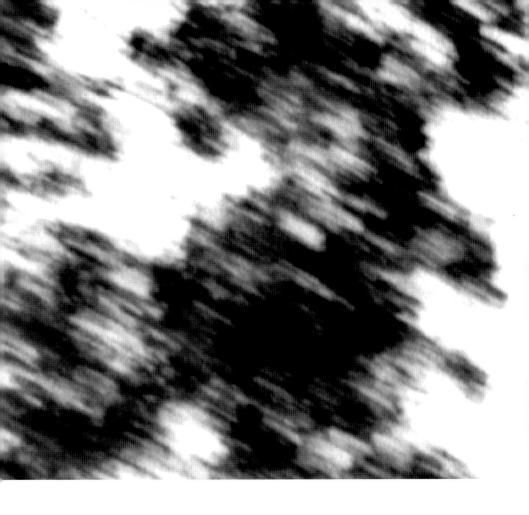

sheets of light. my eyes open slowly. a floating city extends around me. vehicles of the air glide through the skies. I am younger. I remember. I see forward and backward. seconds. years. all experiences are visible. all memories and destinies are present.

THE HIDDEN INFINITIES by Gustavo Alberto Garcia Vaca

Produced by Alma Villegas
Art direction and design by Hideki Nakajima
Published by chamanvision: www.chamanvision.com
Printed and bound in Japan by Toppan Printing Co., Ltd.

ISBN 0-9749357-1-9

All stories and images Copyright © 2006 Gustavo Alberto Garcia Vaca. All rights reserved. No part of this book may be reproduced in any form or by any means without the written permission of the publisher.

The Hidden Infinities is written and illustrated by writer/visual artist Gustavo Alberto Garcia Vaca, the creator of the critically-acclaimed Interstellar Transmissions book. His writing is published in science fiction/cyberpunk/slipstream journals, books and literary anthologies including Dance the Guns to Silence. His artwork is exhibited in art galleries and museums around the world, including the Museum of Emerging Science and Innovation in Tokyo, Japan and the American Cinematheque in Los Angeles, California. His photography is published in the Graffiti World: Street Art from Five Continents art book.
He collaborates visually with Detroit Techno record labels Los Hermanos and Jeff Mills' Axis Records; Francois K's Deep Space dub record label; and others.

Thank you:
The spirits throughout the Universe, mami, nuestras familias, Jeff Mills, Mike Banks, Yoko Uozumi, Axis Records,
Hideki Nakajima, Yuta, Kiyoshi Takami, Thomas Hummel, Ikuo Hikida, Toppan Printing, Dex, Gerald Mitchell, Santi,
Los Hermanos, Ade Mainor, Isela, Bridgette, Submerge, Juan Atkins, Metroplex, Ray 7, DJ 3000, Underground Resistance,
Alice Coltrane, Michelle Coltrane-Carbonell, Jowcol Music, Dego McFarlane, 4 hero, Crewest Gallery, Kiwamu Omae,
Kaze magazine, Ishizaki, Rie, Maria, Underground Gallery, Chifu, Ume, Mita, Disk Union Shibuya, Keiko Hoshikawa,
Cisco Techno Shop, Kenji Kajimura, Shinichiro, Soundscape, Francois K, Aurelie, Wave Music / Deep Space Media,
Art Crimes, Yasuhiro Nara, soph.net, Pedro Alonzo, Trucatriche, Art Data, la familia Trochez, la familia Mazón, la familia Ortiz,
the Cole/Ernsdorf family, the Brechtel family, the Omae family, Chaz Bojorquez, Christina Ochoa, nina, Kozo, Sumika,
Nicholas Ganz, John Carr, CWC Tokyo, Rodrigo Salazar, Takeshi Mochida, Akira, Ken Hayafune, Ashton, Justin, Emiko,
Tamori, Yuka Ohashi, Brent Rollins, Ishiura Masaru, Maryline, Julien, Gonzague, Rafael Castro, strange horizons, dark planet,
project jericho, Kadija Sesay, Nii Ayikwei Parkes, Greg Goodman, Gwen, the American Cinematheque,
the Museum of Emerging Science and Innovation,
all the writers / music artists / visual artists whose work is a source of inspiration, and to you.